T0132062

Buzz hum, buzz hum

Buzz hum, buzz, hum hum hum

How Butterbees™
Came to Bee

by **Lana Bloch & Tania Bloch**   Illustrated by **David Michener**
with additional verse by **Donna Michener**

Special acknowledgements to:

Our late parents, Solomon and Joyce Bloch, for their love and support. Our sister Diane, for her exceptional generosity. Our brothers, David and Jonathon, for their encouragement.

Our cousin, Simon for his loyalty and expert consulting. Karen Grencik, for her creative editing and dedication. David and Donna Michener for believing in our vision. Our illustrator, David Michener passed away in 2018. We dedicate this Butterbees Edition to him and for his mastery in film, animation and illustration.

Lana's children, Adi and Shalev for their love.

Beloved Sadhguru, for his wisdom and showing us how to be.

To order additional copies of this book, contact:
Xlibris
844-714-8691
www.Xlibris.com
Orders@Xlibris.com

ISBN: 978-1-6698-7083-8 (sc)
ISBN: 978-1-6698-7084-5 (e)

Print information available on the last page

Rev. date: 04/17/2023

Dedicated to all the children of the world and to our gifted illustrator, David Michener 1932-2018

Benjamin Franklin Award for Best First Book • iParenting Media Award

Bee Calm

One magical, calm, spring day,
In red rock canyons far away,
Bright butterflies and buzzing bees,
Greeted cacti, flowers, and trees.

Buzz hum, buzz hum, buzz, hum hum hum

On this bright and sunny day,
A bee went out to work and play.
Buzzing happily in the sun,
Flower to flower, having fun.

Buzz hum, buzz hum, buzz, hum hum hum

A handsome butterfly floated by,
Curious to see what's up, and why.
"Little Miss Bee, what is your name?
What are you doing, playing a game?"

Buzz hum, buzz hum, buzz, hum hum hum

Bee Happy

Buzz hum, buzz hum, buzz, hum hum hum

"My friends call me Bonnie Bee.
  I'm as busy as I can be.
I carry pollen to and fro.
  This helps the baby flowers grow.

Buzz hum, buzz hum, buzz, hum hum hum

I collect nectar for the hive,
  Making honey to stay alive.
We keep our beehive neat and clean,
  And work together for our Queen."

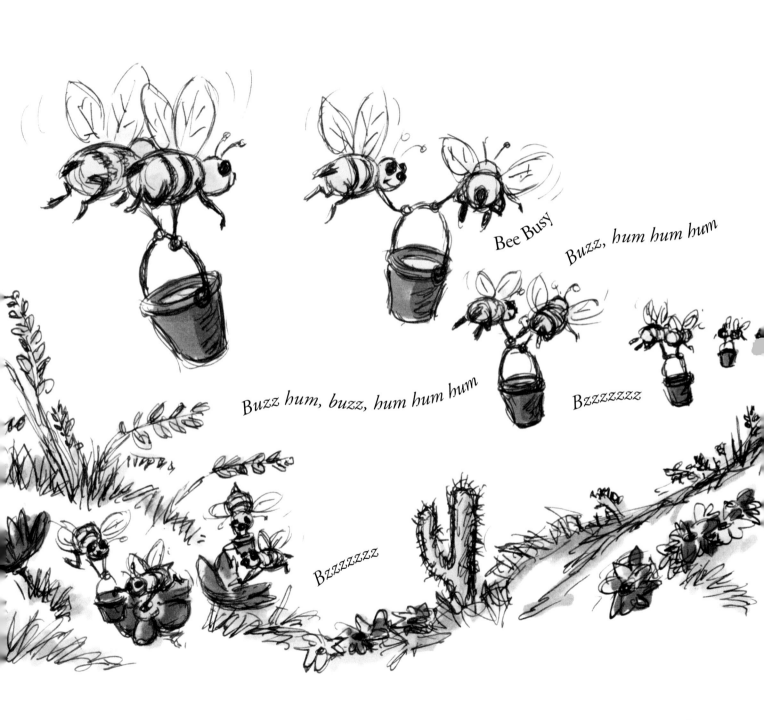

Bee Busy

Buzz, hum hum hum

Buzz hum, buzz, hum hum hum

Bzzzzzzz

Bzzzzzzz

"Enough about me,
    how about you?
What's your name,
    and what do you do?"

"They call me
        Benny Butterfly.
I'm really sort of
        humble and shy."

"I'm a caterpillar at the start,
But we butterflies are very smart.

Bee Smart

A silken chrysalis we learn to spin,
To keep us safe and warm within.

While inside, we gently change form,
So that new butterflies can be born."

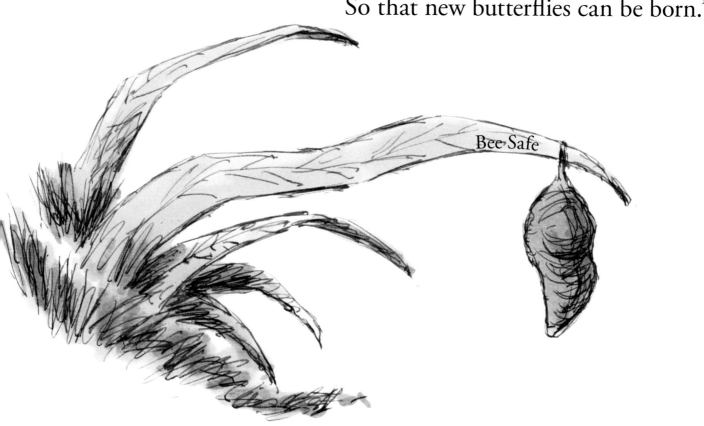

Bee Safe

"When I awake from this deep sleep,
From my chrysalis I slowly creep.

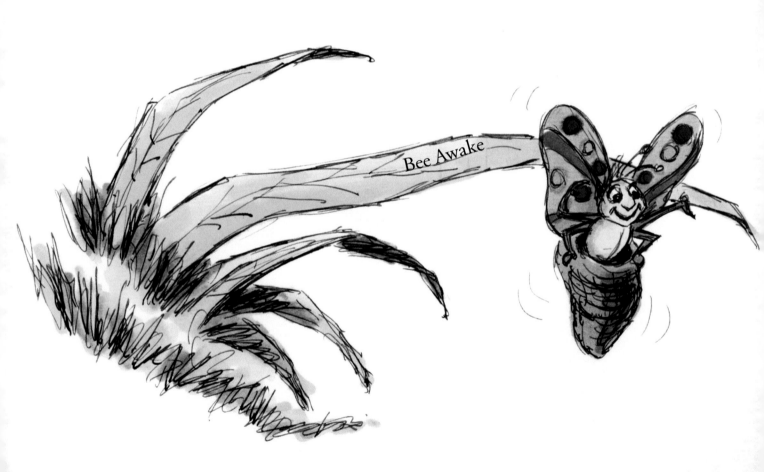

Bee Awake

I spread my wings out
as they dry,
And begin my life
as a butterfly.

Bonnie, you may not
believe all this,
It's called a
met-a-mor-pho-sis!"

Bee Alive

They played as friends, dancing in the sun,
Sharing stories, games, and having fun.
From that day on, they met each day,
Becoming best friends in every way.

Buzz hum, buzz hum, buzz, hum hum hum

Buzz hum, buzz, hum hum hum

Bee Friendly

But one spring day they played past five,
Way past the curfew of the hive.
"Oh, Benny, I'm worried about my Queen,
When she's mad, she's really mean!"

Buzz hum, buzz hum, buzz, hum hum hum

Quickly, Bonnie made a beeline home,
Hoping her queen had left her throne.
Perhaps she could slip into the hive,

But . . .

Buzz hum, buzz hum, buzz, hum hum

Bee Prompt

. . . Guard Bees waited,
not one but *five*!

Off they took her to see the Queen,
Who scolded Bonnie and made a scene.
"Bonnie, why are you so late?
Now I must decide your fate!"

Buzz hum, buzz hum, buzz, hum hum hum

Bonnie was in a terrible fix,
Since butterflies and bees should not mix.
But, she was honest about her day.
Telling the truth was the only way.

"Although I am proud you did not lie,
You must be punished and you know why.

You are now grounded, back in the hive,
To sweep, clean and dust, from five to five!

You'll sleep in the drone cells alone at night.
Guard Bees! Take her from my sight!"

Bzzzzzzz

21

Meanwhile . . .

. . . Worried and sad,
    Benny flew to the creek,
Waiting . . . day by day,
    week by week.

Benny asked his friends,
    "What should I do?"
Rolf Rattlesnake hissed,
    "I haven't a clue!"

But Uqualla Quail,
    known to be wise,
Noticed the sadness
    in Benny's eyes.

"Be patient," she said,
        "follow your heart.
Listen inside
        to your knowing part."

Buzz hum, buzz, hum hum hum

Bee Free

Then it came, the sweetest song,
      One he'd not heard, for, oh, so long.
      "Could it be my Bonnie Bee,
      Is once again, buzzing free!"

Buzz hum, buzz hum, buzz, hum hum hum

"Oh, Bonnie, how I've missed you so,
      Seeing you sets my heart aglow."
"Oh, Benny, I have missed you too,
      Afraid I'd never again find you."

They flew to their place by the creek,
Taking the time to share and speak.
Benny suggested with a smile,
"Let's just sit and be still awhile."

Benny listened to his knowing part,
And heard the words, *"Follow your heart."*
He whispered, "Bonnie, will you be mine?"
"Oh, yes," she sighed, "till the end of time."

Buzz hum, buzz hum, buzz, hum hum hum

Bee Caring

All creatures and rocks smiled to see,
These two wed in love's harmony.
Uqualla Quail, standing proud and tall,
Sounded her love song marriage call.

Bee Loving

Then one day to their utmost joy . . .

Bee Joyful

. . . Butterbees were born, a girl and boy!
They named them Bizzy and Buzzy,
Both so cute, cuddly, and fuzzy.

With bee bodies and butterfly wings,
Babee butterbees are amazing things!

Buzz hum, buzz hum, buzz, hum hum hum

Uqualla took them to her heart,
    Wanting the babees to have the best start.
She took them under her loving wing,
    Telling wise tales that life can bring.

She said . . .

"Inside there is a knowing place,
Where lives the soul
and loving grace.

It helps us when
we're feeling sad,
To know these feelings
aren't so bad.

It helps us see
others as they are,
Accepting all creatures,
near and far."

Bee Accepting

33

The Queen got word
of what Uqualla said.
Thoughts went 'round and 'round
in her head.

One day she awoke,
as from a dream,
The Queen felt happy,
not quite so mean.

She'd always loved
Bonnie in her heart,
And felt it was time
to make a new start.

The Queen had
     a happy and smiling face,
Now that she'd found
          her own knowing place.

Hearing the news
     of the Butterbees' birth,
She began to dance
     with glee and mirth.

So . . .
That's the tale of how we came to bee,
Bizzy and Buzzy Butterbee.
We float like butterflies, buzz like bees,
Pollinate flowers, cacti, and trees.

Buzz hum, buzz hum, buzz, hum hum hum

We gather pollen in pollen sacs,
    And fix our home with strong beeswax.
We spin silk, make honey, and sweet bee bread,
    And collect nectar till time for bed.

We bet you're blessed with talents, too.
    Why don't you try to name a few?"

Bee
Creative

Bee Kind

"*Hive 'n Seek* is our favorite game,
  Finding 'Bee ways' that we can name.
Bee helpful and wise, bee loving and true.
    Bee happy, bee kind, and just bee you!"

Buzz hum, buzz hum, buzz, hum hum hum

As the golden sun sets in the west,
It's once again time for all to rest.

Bizzy and Buzzy lay down to sleep,
Hugging each other with love so deep.
Drifting in night's sweet wonderlands,
Humming this prayer and holding hands . . .
"Whatever happens to you and me,
Help us to bee the best we can bee."

Buzz hum, buzz hum, buzz, hum hum hum

Shhh . . . Bee still . . .
you may hear the hum.

Just Bee You!

Buzz hum, buzz hum, buzz, hum hum hum

Benny
Butterfly

Bonnie
Bee

Buzz hum, buzz hum, buzz, hum hum hum

Buzz hum,

Queen

Rolf
Rattlesnake

Bizzy
Butterbee

Buzzy
Butterbee

Buzz hum, buzz hum, buzz, hum hum hum

Bye, bye from us all,
And let's bee friends!

Rumpledink
Rabbit

Uqualla
Quail

About the Authors

LANA BLOCH and TANIA BLOCH are sisters and colleagues. The Butterbees were born from their love of Sedona, bees, butterflies and children. The children's book was originally self published in 2002, by their former small business, Bee Unlimited.

They have decided to reprint this edition, to honor the "Butterbees" gifted illustrator, David Michener, who passed away in 2018.

During Covid, the sisters moved to live in a little blue cottage in Isha Enclave, located at the Isha Foundation, Institute for Inner Sciences, Tennessee. Isha is a beautiful, rural community founded by Sadhguru, to enhance wellbeing and human consciousness, through the tools of yoga and meditation.

The sisters vision for the "Butterbees", is to empower children to tap into their unique gifts and talents and to value one another's differences.

About the Illustrator

DAVID MICHENER was a key artist for Walt Disney Studios until his retirement in 1987. He passed away on February 15th, 2018. A serendipitous meeting between neighbors, led to Davids last artistic collaboration, as the illustrator for, How Butterbees Came to Bee.

David taught at California Institute of the Arts in Valencia, hoping to inspire young artists with his love of animation and film.

He and his wife Donna, were married for over 60 years, with 3 daughters and 6 grandchildren, all of whom are very proud of his many talents.

Printed in the United States
by Baker & Taylor Publisher Services